Friendship Takes Courage

Ofir Mor

ISBN: 149276728X
ISBN-13: 13:978-1492767282

DOWNLOAD FOR FREE

A high resolution 70x50 poster image
+
Cool desktop background images at:

FriendshipTakesCourage.com

CONTENTS

The water-cano fields

The all knowing book gorm

The Forest of Courage

The brave Knight

The frightened sand gopher

Aaoo aaah!!

CHAPTER 1
Planet Water-Bright

Far far away in a magical place in space,
there was a beautiful planet called Water-
Bright. It had a magical heart
made of light.

Water-Bright was named for the way it was made. On the surface, there were a few islands floating, but underneath, it was all made of water.

A magical light shone through the water from the planet's heart and touched the hearts of all beings on the planet.

Yet the heart was sad, and its light was fading away.

Why do you think it was sad?

Once, all its creatures lived in wonderful harmony and friendship. The magical heart's sweet loving light was shining through the water, embracing all living beings on the planet.

But for much longer than a long long time, the beings of Water-Bright had been used to feeling the heart's love and took it for granted. They stopped being brave and felt no need to share the love they had with each other. And so the magical heart of light became sad and dim.

When Water-Bright lost its magical light, all fell into chaos. The bravest beings became angry, the happiest became sad, and they lost their purple and most of their green.

All had forgotten how to be brave and had forgotten who they were.

The flying hug bugs were not falling in love with each other, or with trees, or with... anything hugable.

The silly flower rabbits became too shy to do silly things and show their silly faces.

The lazy gophers, were and remain a lazy bunch. And still, they used to turn into hard-workers in their sleep. Just for a few moments they would climb trees, look for the perfect spot to lie down and make sure it was clean and tidy all around. Now... they are simply too lazy all the time.

In the hopes of restoring courage, friendship and magic to the planet, the heart waited for the most special day to arrive. On such a magical day, special kinds of beings are born.

Water-Bright has five small suns circling around it, so there's always light, there is no night. When the light from all five small suns lined up as a smile, above the Water-Cano fields, the magical heart gave birth to Joy.

CHAPTER 2
Joy

Joy was born through the biggest
Water-Cano in Water- Bright and he was a
very wise boy who knew all about courage
and friendship.
He was highly sensitive too and could
feel the deepest feelings of others around
him as though they were his own.
More than anything Joy needed friends
to love, and to be loved. He was eager
to help others overcome fear and make
friendships.

Sliding down from the highest Water-Cano might seem like a scary thing to do, but Joy was not afraid of heights. He was not afraid of falling or failing. His only real fear was losing a friend.

After a joyous slide down the Water-Cano, Joy's feet touched the ground. He lifted his eyes to the sky and smiled to the five suns who smiled right back at him.

Magical grass frogs were boooing all around him, each booo carrying a powerful magic. when you are boooed at, you feel like you belong, when they say booo you simply feel like you're home.

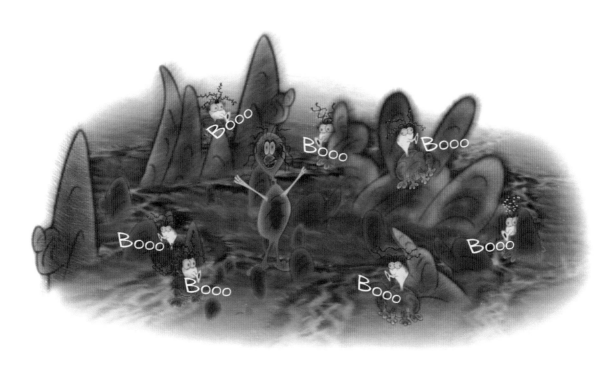

Joy was cheerful seeing the path curving ahead. Thoughts of the adventure that awaited him and the friendships he would make filled him with excitement.

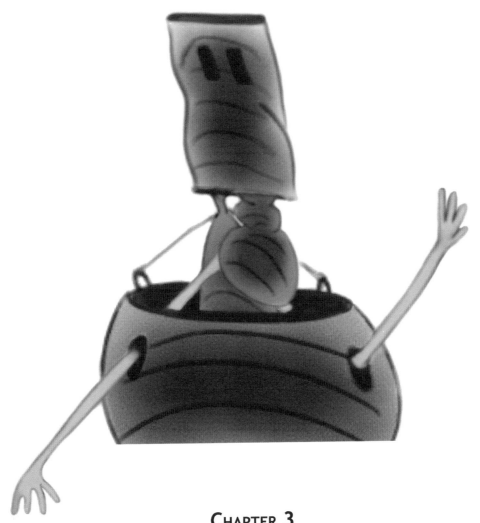

CHAPTER 3
Whistling and Noses

No matter the shape, if it's big or
small, pink and blue or round as a ball.
If it's sticky like honey or soft like a
bunny.
A nose is simply a nose, and if you like
it, it's a beautiful nose.

Joy began walking down the path away from the Water-Cano fields in search of a friend. He reached a field of colourful flowers and water trees. Tiny hug bugs were flying around with no purpose at all. A few silly flower rabbits were hiding behind rocks, and lazy gophers were laying around being lazy.

As he entered the path to the field he heard a voice behind a water tree attempting to sound serious:

"Princess! I swear to protect you. I will always be there for you." He got closer and saw a figure dressed as a knight holding a broom. There was nobody next to him, but he kept talking to himself as if someone was there, repeating

himself as he tried to find the right words.

"Princess!" The knight became nervous. For a moment he forgot what he was about to say. "Princess! I am a brave knight. I offer myself to serve you!" The brave knight seemed displeased with these words and tried again: "Beautiful princess, finally we meet, I wish to be your brave knight!"

At that moment Joy approached the brave knight and said hello.

The brave knight was so busy rehearsing. He did not notice little Joy and was startled. With his helmet on he could barely see what was next to him, and he spoke with a nervous stutter:

"Are you - are you - a princess?"

"I don't know...what's a princess?" Joy replied.

The brave knight lowered his head with sadness. "Ho, never mind" he mumbled. Then he raised his head, took a deep breath and said, "If you were a princess I would say this: Beautiful princess! I am so happy to have met you! I am a brave knight and wish to be at your side!"

The two had a silent moment and the brave knight asked, "Well, what do you think? Will she like me? It is a well-known fact that princesses love brave knights."

Joy replied hesitantly. "How can your princess like you if you are hiding behind a mask? She won't be able to see your face."

The knight became silent, thinking over what Joy had said. "You have a good point. But I can't show my face! The truth, if you must know it, is that I am ashamed of my... nose! There! I have said it!" He sobbed.

Then he began to yell. "I hate being a knight!, carrying this heavy weight everywhere I go and the tin can on my head. It's itchy and my nose hurts!"

The brave knight took off the barrel he was wearing and threw it on the ground.

Joy smiled and asked the brave knight, "Is meeting a princess a good thing?"

"Of course it is! It is the most wonderful thing that could ever happen!"

"I happen to know that wonderful things happen only when we listen to our heart," Joy replied.

The brave knight got restless fearing he may never meet his princess. "Are you sure? Well... okay... so I must listen to my heart then, but how?"

"The first thing you must do is be brave," said Joy.

"That's great! I can do that. I have already been a brave knight for a long time. What's next?"

Joy told the knight to close his eyes. He placed his warm hand on his heart and asked, "What makes your heart warm and happy? Do you remember? What is it that you love to do?"

The brave knight took a deep breath. He felt the feeling of warmth and he realised he had not felt it in a long time. Suddenly, he burst into tears. They were tears of joy.

He threw his helmet and raised his voice.

"I remember! I remember what makes my heart warm and happy!"

It's when I whistle!

He began to whistle, and as the knight whistled all of the silly flower rabbits came out from hiding with the silliest smiles on their faces.

All of the lazy gophers woke up, stood on their feet and danced a lazy slow fun dance. And all the flying hug bugs began hugging each other. One hug bug fell in-love with the knight's nose.

By the end of the whistle all the creatures around Joy and the brave knight were deeply moved, except for the lazy gophers who got tired of standing and fell into a deep sleep. One flying hug bug hugged the brave knight's nose and would not let go.

"That was magical!" said Joy, "And I think your nose is beautiful!."
The brave knight still had his doubts about his nose, but he felt so happy that he couldn't be bothered thinking about it.

I feel so light! I feel so happy! From now on, I am no longer a brave knight, but a happy whistler!

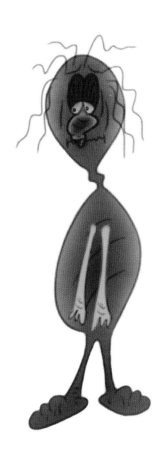

CHAPTER 4
Friendship

A good friend will be there when you are
sad and blue.
When you are in a jam and your head
is stuck on glue.
It's best when your friends nose is big
and chunky.
And if your first friend is pink you are
sooooooo lucky!

Suddenly fear came over Joy. It began to spread through his body. His hands were shaking, and he could not look in Whistler's eyes.

"What's wrong, Joy?" asked Whistler.

Now, it was Joy's turn to stammer and be nervous. "Do you...do you want to be my friend?"

"A friend? Yes! I like the sound of that! I have never had a friend before. Actually, what do friends do?"

"Well..." Joy hesitated. "Friends care for each other. When they are away they sometimes miss one another. When they meet they feel love in their hearts. They love to share their deepest feelings, and sometimes they feel like hugging."

"I like that!" said Whistler.

But are friends there for each other even when it's scary?

Especially when it's scary!

"Then I would like to share something with you Joy. I am still ashamed of my nose. I am nervous that when I meet the princess she won't like it, although I am not as nervous as I was before."

Joy was still unsure of what a princess was and said, "I have a feeling princesses love noses like yours. I would like to share something with you too, I am very happy to have you as my new friend."

"Me too!" said Whistler.

The two friends were so moved that they had to give each other a hug.

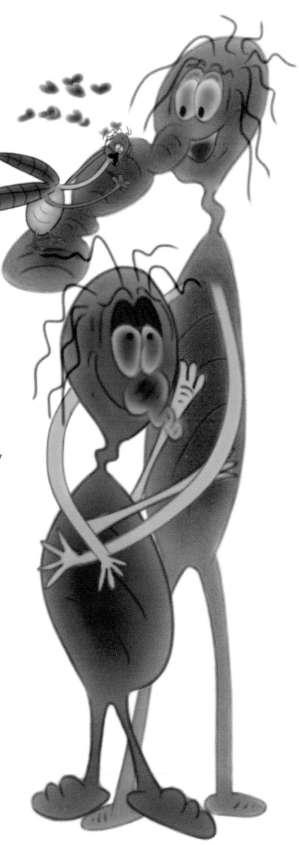

CHAPTER 5
The All Knowing
Book Gorm

The five suns were no longer together in the sky. The only one remaining was the sun of silliness. Its heart is yellow and it has silly brown rays of light. It reminds all beings not to take themselves too seriously and, if possible, to simply do something really silly.

The two new friends walked up the path, discussing friendship, noses and silly things.

"What do you suppose is sillier?" asked Whistler, "Sticking a finger in the nose or a foot in the mouth?"

Joy was pondering
over what a good question
it was, but before he could
think of an answer, a third
figure appeared.

He seemed exhausted, barely moving as he tried to drag a huge basket, a basket filled with many books. He was so busy attempting to move the heavy load that he did not notice that the two friends were already next to him.

"Hello! I am Joy." The figure turned his head, his eyes looking up eagerly.

"Do either of you have a book??" Joy and Whistler shook their heads and he continued on quickly:

"I am a serious book gorm. It's so good to see you! I was hoping to meet someone today so that I could share the many things that I know! The first thing I would like you to know is that I am smart! So, so smart! I know everything! Yes! I know everything there is to know."

The book gorm suddenly froze as he noticed Whistler's nose. "That's a beautiful nose. Can I touch it?"

Whistler blushed, and as the book gorm reached his hand towards his nose, the flying hug bug got angry. He would not share the nose with anyone, so the book gorm moved his attention back to how smart he was.

"Yes! I am smart! Now ask me anything you want to know!"

The book gorm jumped on his book basket excitedly, looking like a mad gorm as he yelled and hopped about.

Everything about anything!!..

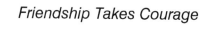

Anything about everything!!..

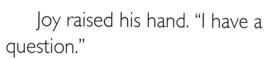

Joy raised his hand. "I have a question."

The book gorm became silent. He jumped to the ground with anticipation, leaned over and listened carefully.

"Can you tell me what it feels like to feel love?" Joy asked.

The book gorm froze again and seemed a bit shocked but went on answering anyway.

"Of course I can!" He placed his hands on his head and seemed to be thinking hard on the matter.

"It's in my head! It will come to me! You will see! I am smart!"

The two friends waited for a few moments as the book gorm thought really, really hard.

Suddenly he jumped back on his feet. "Don't move! Just wait! I will find it!" Then, he bounced into his basket and began tossing books all around.

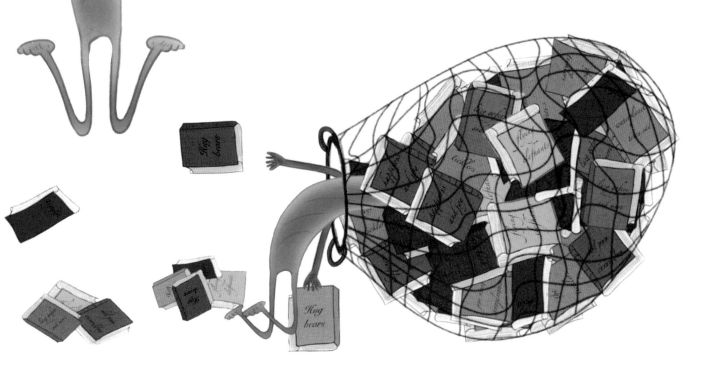

A few moments later, the entire book collection was scattered on the ground.

The gorm turned back to Joy slowly. He got down on his knees with tears in his eyes and begged, "Please, please, please, tell me the answer! I must know!"

Joy felt the gorm's sadness. He placed his hand on his heart and said, "Love is not something you can explain with your head. The only way to know love is to feel it.

Do you feel that warmth in your heart now? When was the last time you felt that warmth?"

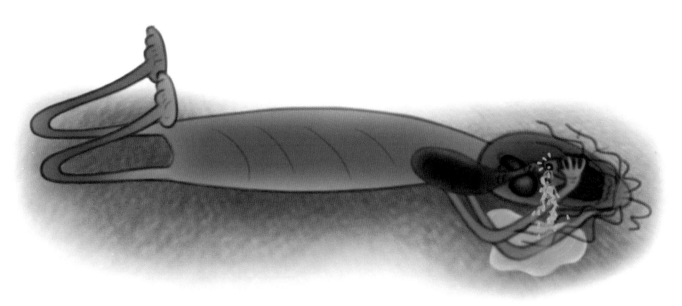

Tiny tears formed in the gorm's eyes, and grew bigger until he laid on the ground and a river of tears flowed from his eyes. When there were no more tears left, he spoke sadly.

"When I was a young gorm, I did not care for knowing everything. All I cared about, what truly made me happy, were those fluffy, soft, silly flower rabbits. They climbed onto me and I hugged them all day. They had the silliest faces. I laughed so much and felt love in my heart.

I was ashamed of my silliness and became too serious. All I cared for was knowing everything and being serious. Life was so much simpler and full of joy when I had silliness around me."

Whistler remembered how lonely he had been when he forgot who he was and said, "But now that you feel your heart again, maybe those silly flower rabbits will come back!"

The gorm felt a bit of hope. "Do you think so? You think they will come back to me?"

Joy smiled. "Yes, in fact I know exactly what can bring them back! First, you will have to do something really, really silly."

Joy smiled at
Whistler and asked
him to whistle.

As Whistler whistled and the gorm jammed his foot in his mouth, the sun of silliness seemed even sillier. The lazy gophers woke up and felt like doing something silly too. So they stood on one foot right before they dropped on the ground and fell back into a deep sleep.

The flying hug bugs felt like hugging each other.

Many fluffy silly flower rabbits began popping up from every direction with the silliest smiles on their faces.

As they saw the gorm being silly with his heart open for love, they silly skipped towards him.

There were so many that came, and the gorm was covered from head to toe with silly rabbits. You could see nothing but rabbits and the gorm's happy smile.

"From now on I am Gorm the silly!", he said with happiness.

Whistler felt excited. He looked at Joy and said, "Now that Gorm feels love in his heart, he can be our new friend!

Will you join us on our adventure? Will you be our new friend?"

Gorm the silly looked so happy. "You mean that not only my silly, fluffy friends came back, but I also have two new friends?"

Hooray!

As the sun of laziness began to rise, the three friends felt lazy and tired. Every time this sun would rise, all any one felt like doing was absolutely nothing.

Doing absolutely nothing, the creatures of Water-Bright would ask themselves, "What's good about that?" But they would always become too lazy to think of an answer and fell asleep instead.

And so, Gorm, Whistler and Joy all fell into a deep, lazy sleep.

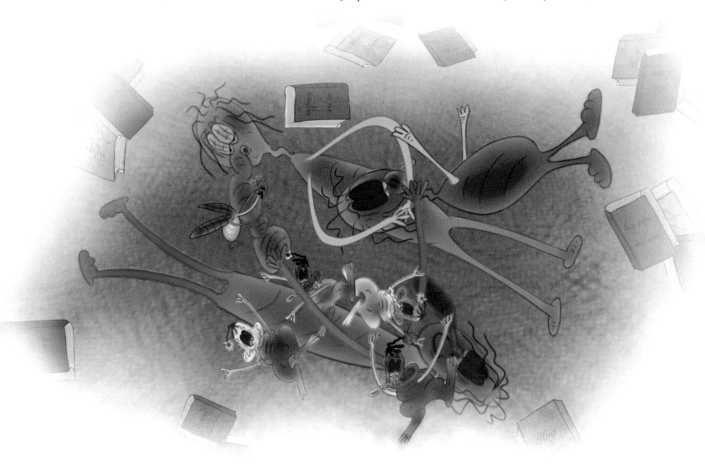

CHAPTER 6

Brave Bouncies and a Frightened Sand Gopher

By the time Joy, Whistler and Gorm woke up, the sun of courage was high in the sky. When it shines, the beings of Water-Bright feel their fears the strongest. At the same time, it inspires them to overcome their fears and be courageous.

When the three friends opened their eyes, many lazy gophers were cuddling with them. They seemed to like cuddling with someone who was not only a lazy gopher.

They were also very fond of Gorm's books, thinking that they made great beds and blankets. A silly flower rabbit stayed with Gorm, and a flying hug bug was still stuck on Whistler's nose.

Gorm picked up one of the books, a magical book that tells you everything about where ever you are. He promised his silly little friend that he will never be too serious again. As for the rest of the books, he decided they would probably be much more useful to the lazy gophers.

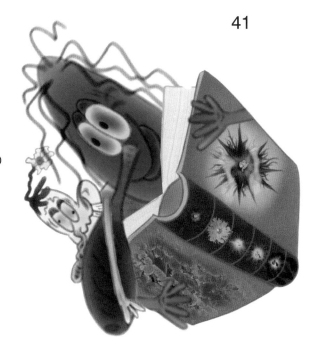

Many silly flower rabbits popped up on the rocks by the side of the path, waving at Gorm with silly smiles.

"I feel so happy," said Gorm. "All that silliness, I missed it so much, and I love having you two as my friends."

Gorm was overwhelmed and could hardly speak.

All three friends were so moved they had to stop and give each other a hug before they could move ahead.

The three friends then began walking up the path, looking forward to what lay ahead.

"Do you really think I have a beautiful nose?" asked Whistler. Gorm nodded his head. "I have seen many kinds of noses in my life, and your nose is not only beautiful, it's also the most special nose I have ever seen!"

"S-p-e-c-i-a-l," Whistler repeated the word slowly, not fully knowing what it meant. "I like that!"

Inspired by the sun of courage, Whistler shared with his new friends his tales of bravery:

"Once, when the sun of courage was high in the sky like today, I stood under a tree filled with lazy, sleepy gophers, even though they were all asleep and could have fallen on me at any time!"

"Woah!" said Gorm, who knew very well the dangers of lazy gophers falling from a tree in their sleep. "Were you scared?"

"Yes!" Whistler seemed proud. "But I was also brave, and I was brave again when I took off my knight's armour and revealed my nose. So were you, Gorm, when you acted silly!" Gorm felt brave as well as happy.

The path took them downhill. While they discussed laziness, noses and bravery, another figure appeared. His back was bent low, and he held a heavy barrel behind him. Shivering with fear, he did not see the three companions as they approached him from behind.

"Hello!" called Joy with a smile. Whistler was about to speak when the frightened creature screamed. His face turned pale and he quickly jumped into his barrel.

Aaaaaaaaah!!

"Who is there???" He called timidly. "Are you small? With one foot maybe?"

The three friends looked at each other in confusion. "I'm not small," said Whistler.

"Neither am I," said Gorm.

Joy raised his hand. "I am a bit small. Is that a bad thing?"

The frightened creature mumbled and then asked, "Well, are you bouncing on one foot and do you love kicking?"

The three friends looked at Joy's feet and shook their heads "No, I have two feet," said Joy. "And I don't like kicking." The frightened creature raised the top of his head and took a frightened sneak peak before hopping out of his barrel and immediately clinged on to it.

Gorm opened his book. "I have seen that creature in my book before. Yes! That is a frightened sand gopher!"

Whistler scratched his head. "Is he also lazy?"

"No," said Gorm. "A sand gopher is bigger then a lazy gopher. They love to dig in the sand and tend to be frightened of everything for no reason at all."

For a good reason!

They are everywhere and they will kick you!

Who is kicking?

Do they
kick noses?

What about silly
flower rabbits?

Whistler and Gorm shivered, and the frightened sand gopher sighed.

"My sand village is behind the scariest forest in Water-Bright, the Forest of Courage. Because I am the bravest sand gopher in my village, I must venture out across the forest, so that I can come back every day and tell the rest of the gophers how scary it is out there.

Every time I cross the forest, they come. They are everywhere! When you look forward, they come from behind. When you look to one side, they come from the other. You don't know where they are until they kick! Where, you ask?" The Sand gopher became sad "Where it's already so sore that I can't take it anymore!"

On my bottom!

"That's not very nice," said Whistler.

"No, it's not!" Gorm agreed.

The frightened sand gopher nodded his head. "That is why you should carry a barrel with you at all times, and keep it tight and close to your behind!"

"I can help you!" said Joy. The frightened gopher paused.

"You will enter the Forest of Courage with me? Will you make them stop?"

"Yes." said Joy. "But only if you are willing to be brave."

Not at all sure if he could be brave at that moment, the frightened gopher paused again and took his time with the decision.

He shivered and shivered and finally said, "I will be b-brave."

And so Whistler, Gorm, Joy, and the frightened sand gopher approached the entrance of the Forest of Courage.

Facing the dark entrance made Whistler and Gorm very scared. Joy felt their fear and became frightened too, but not from the dark forest or the kicking. He wondered if his friends would join him or leave when they were afraid.

They all froze with fear. Joy looked at his friends and felt sadness. But then, Whistler spoke up.

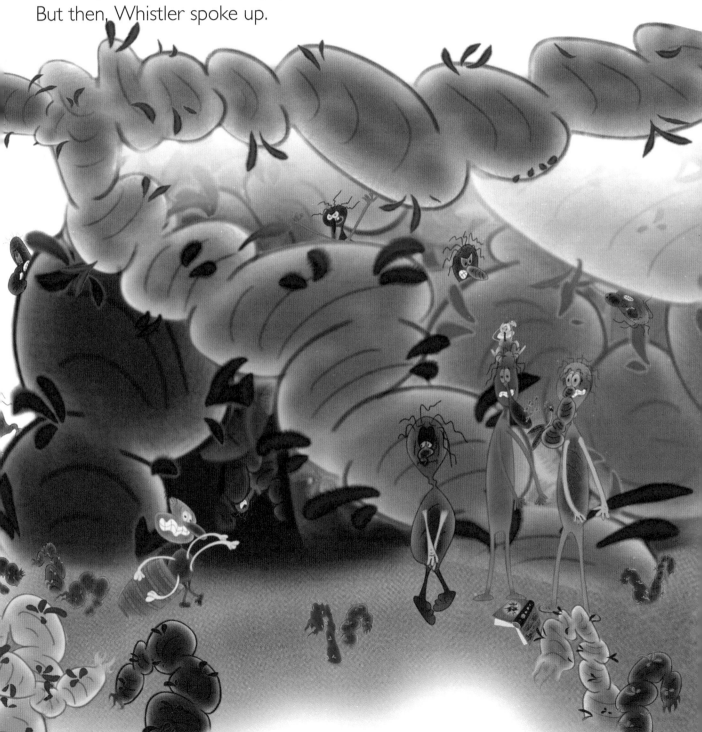

Friends are there for each other even when it's scary!

"Yes, they are!" Gorm agreed with pride.

Joy's heart was overwhelmed with happiness and love for his companions, but this was not the time for hugging. Gorm opened his magical book and began to read:

"Longer than a long time ago, Courage Tree Forest had the tallest trees in all of Water-Bright. They were so tall, they reached the clouds. They were so tall that no one would dare climb them, no one, except for the brave bouncies.

The brave boucies were the most courageous beings in Water-Bright. Even though they were small and had only one foot, they would still do what no being in all of Water-Bright dared to do.

For the trees to grow, they needed to feel the bouncies brave tiny hearts.

When the sun of courage was above the forest, the brave bouncies climbed the trees and bounced bravely from one tree to another. The trees felt their courage, and became taller and taller until they reached the clouds.

The brave bouncies kept climbing higher and higher, and when they reached the top of the trees, their tiny hearts felt so much courage that they all yelled, "Weeeeeeeeee!" as they bounced from one tree to another.

When the trees of courage sensed the courage in their beloved bouncies' tiny hearts, their flowers opened up and spread a magical powder of courage through the winds to all of Water-Bright, inspiring bravery in all beings.

But longer than a long time ago, many outsiders entered the forest with fear in their hearts. The brave bouncies could not stand for fear in their forest, and they turned into angry bouncies.

All they cared for now was to find someone frightened in their forest who they could kick in the bottom.

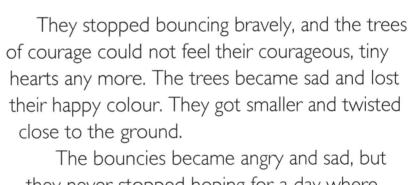

They stopped bouncing bravely, and the trees of courage could not feel their courageous, tiny hearts any more. The trees became sad and lost their happy colour. They got smaller and twisted close to the ground.

The bouncies became angry and sad, but they never stopped hoping for a day where someone courageous would enter the forest so they could feel courage in their hearts, bounce bravely on their beloved trees and "Weeeeeeeeee" once again."

The four companions entered the dark forest, and as they got deeper and deeper, they began hearing whispers all around them.

The frightened gopher's legs shivered and he mumbled to himself, "Please please not my butt. Please not again."

Whistler whispered to his friends, "I am scared."

"Me too" said Gorm.

The silly flower rabbit hid behind Gorm's legs, and the hug bug, well, he was so busy falling in love with Whistler's nose that he did not notice a thing.

Joy held Whistler's hand and said, "The only thing to do when there's fear is to be brave. We need you to be brave my dear friend. We need you to be courageous and whistle."

Whistler took a deep breath and felt fear in his body. He took two more and finally began whistling a brave whistle.

His whistle had a sweet sweet sound. The trees felt courage they had not felt for a long time and began to move. Gorm calmed down, but the sand gopher was still frightened.

Out of nowhere, four bouncies appeared. They were all small, one of them smaller than the rest and one bigger than the others. He was the chief of the angry bouncies. They seemed to be really angry.

It's the tiny red one!!!

Aaaaaaaaah!!!

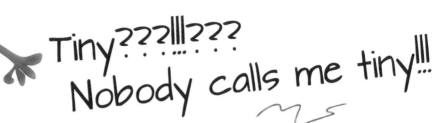

Tiny???..!!!???
Nobody calls me tiny!!!

The chief bouncy pointed at Joy. "You!
You are the first one not to be afraid for
a long, long time...but, your friends are!
Especially that Frightened gopher! You
brought fear into our forest. This is
outrageous!, We won't stand for it!"

Joy smiled and spoke to the chief bouncie. "Will you grant us a tiny moment to overcome fear and be courageous?"

The chief bouncy became grumpy and mumbled to himself.

"A tiny moment, you say?

We will have to discuss this amongst ourselves."

Four more bouncies appeared, and they all cuddled in a circle to debate Joy's request. Finally, a few moments passed and the chief bouncy turned back to Joy.

"We miss bouncing bravely on our beloved trees, bouncing and weeeeeeeing with courage in our tiny brave hearts. We are so tired of kicking, and most of all, we are tired of feeling angry."

The chief bouncy paused and looked at the smallest bouncy. "Well...except Naughty Bouncy. He likes kicking."

"We have agreed to give you your tiny moment because you are brave."

Joy turned to the sand gopher and asked him to come out of his barrel. "Close your eyes and take a deep breath. Do you feel the fear in your body? Where do you feel it?"

The sand gopher opened his eyes in panic:

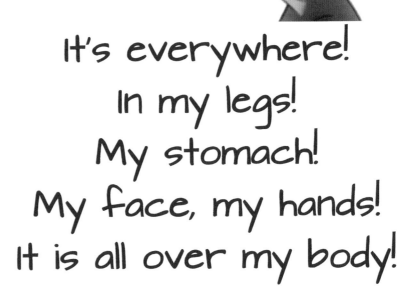

It's everywhere!
In my legs!
My stomach!
My face, my hands!
It is all over my body!

"Now, now," said Joy with a still and calm voice, "Close your eyes, relax your hands and breathe slower. Every time air comes in through your body, say hello to the fear."

The gopher took a few breaths and Whistler and Gorm joined him until his legs stopped shaking and he began to calm down.

Joy continued softly. "Every time the air goes through your body, it says hello to your fear as if he is a friend."

The tiny moment passed, and Whistler looked at Gorm.

The sand gopher opened his eyes and smiled. He bounced bravely on his barrel and raised his hands up high yelling:

The trees of courage shook and began to grow. The chief bouncy bounced on one of the trees and spoke with a loud voice:

"Brave bouncies! We can stop kicking and being angry! We can stop being sad and grumpy! Today we have witnessed true courage!"

All the bouncies in Courage Forest cheered. "Our trees are calling us, It's time to be brave! Bounce higher and higher until we reach the clouds, until our tiny hearts burst with courage and weeeeeeeeeeeee!"

The brave bouncies bounced from one tree to another as the trees stretched up and grew higher and higher. The darkness left the forest and the sun of courage shone brighter than ever before. The edges of the trees disappeared above the clouds and so did the brave bouncies. You could only hear them weeeeeeeeeeeeing from far, far away.

Finally, the flowers of the trees opened up spreading magical powder of courage in all of Water-Bright.

The brave sand gopher thanked Joy and his friends. He felt proud as he left the forest to tell his sand village, and the three friends returned back to the entrance of the forest.

Whistler, Gorm, and Joy all felt exceptionally brave. "I like being brave, it makes me happy!" said Whistler. "Me too," said Gorm, and as they reached the edge of the forest, the chief bouncy appeared with a joyous smile and the young Naughty Bouncy.

"Brave friends, Naughty Bouncy is the bravest among us. He wishes to join you and brings magical powder of courage with him. He needs to bounce bravely every day and promises to be brave and not angry."

Whistler, Gorm and Joy smiled at each other. They felt excited to have a new friend. "Will you be our new friend?" asked Joy.

Naughty Bouncy only said, "Weeeee" as he bounced into Joy's hands.

Whistler turned hesitantly to the chief bouncy. "Do you know of any princesses in your forest?"

"What is a princess?" asked the chief bouncy. "Is that something that bounces bravely on a tree?"

Whistler lowered his head. "No its... ho, never mind."

"I had read once of a place with many princesses!" said Gorm. "It's not here, but it's on another island."

"Really? Where? We must go there!"

"I am sorry my beautiful pink-nosed friend. I do not know."

Joy turned to Whistler. "I promise you my dear friend, that you will meet your princess. All you need to do is keep being brave, happy and true to your heart."

"Ok." Whistler raised his head with hope in his heart and a smile. "I will never feel alone with you as my friends."

Joy smiled. "I am so happy to have all of you as my friends."

Looking down the path ahead, the four friends were so excited about the new adventures that awaited them. Would a new day bring a new friend? A new fear to overcome? Maybe both?

To my brave
niece Ela

The bravest wisest words may simply come out of a young innocent child.
Thank you Ela my brave little niece for inspiring me to step out of the dreamworld, and write you a story.

ACKNOWLEDGMENTS

I thank my father for his support,
my mom for encouraging my creativity
and my chatty neighbor's cat
for making me smile every day
on my way to work.

About The Author

Ofir Mor lives in Tel aviv and in
a dream world.
He is a highly sensitive therapist
with a never-ending desire to help
children and parents find happiness.
At the age of 35, he finally
decided to step out of his imaginary
world to reality with a story.

Free high resolution poster image + cool desktop images at:
FriendshipTakesCourage.com

13373774R00045

Made in the USA
San Bernardino, CA
19 July 2014